The Passing

Paens & Ephemera

Ben Webb

ARC-EN-CIEL EDITIONS
Risking Enchantment, London, 2024

978-1-0687662-0-6

Cover Image: 'Pensador' by Daniel El Dubijo
Design & Typeset by Inkspiral Design

THE PASSING

For Nick Campbell with love

It's like that warm evening you read to me
Both knowing deeply that it's a good time, a good time for us
Thank you, thank you, thank you

YOKO ONO

& in grateful memory of Paul Norman

Oh since my teacher died
I am a student now
Of whom I cannot tell
Of what I cannot tell

DIANE CLUCK

My thanks are due to

Emma Adams, Mike Betts, Matt Bright, Louis Brownhill, Henny & Mark Braund, Nick Campbell, Diane Cluck, Martin Corless-Smith, Daniel El Dubijo, Jenni Fagan, Siobhan Finnegan, Jon Herring, Emily Jeremiah, Imogen Knight, Will Norman, Pip McDonald, Alice Oswald, Danielle O'Leary, Chris Pearse, Viv Ridley, Mariano Ruiz & Jorge Negrete, Rajni Shah, Nick Skerten, Sticky Fingers, Tessa Walker, Brendan Wyer

Alone with our madness and favourite flower
We see that there really is nothing left to write about.
Or rather, it is necessary to write down the same old things
In the same way, repeating the same things over and over
For love to continue and be gradually different.

JOHN ASHBERY

The trouble was not
in the kitchen or the tulips
but only in my head, my head.

ANNE SEXTON

Any characteristic act – whether it's a sailor's sailing or a hermit's withdrawal or a writer's writing – is an act of reciprocal invocation. It activates a world in which the act makes sense. It invents.

LYN HEJINIAN

The Passing

Waking Moment

I don’t know where to begin but

Advice

Every several years
reconsider your pornographies.

Fall asleep with the light on,
let seasons pass.

Walk into the room and say
teach me something new.

Night Affinities

In London, darkness falls; rain pours, we walk.
On Saint Martin's Lane, which isn't what it was,
A man carries his dog. Life goes on.

The Vanishing Lake

Poets disappear
It is a seasonal occurrence
Our work is a rumour
We surprise ourselves

Metamorphoses

Like Daphne, I transformed into a tree,
on the day of the vote, in London, in 2016.
An end to history, an end to myth,
our good name gone, petrified, unblessed.

What we lost then and what might have been.

I'm still here, loving you with words, remembering,
leafless, open-branched, hoping you'll return.

Words

Kindness. Blindness. Monkeys in the branches of the trees along the Seine. Sanity is a manatee that wakes up each morning in its wet blue bed with its right mind on. Right on. Write on. Go long until the words begin to learn a new grammar. Let words do what they want to do, and words will teach you kindness and a kind of patience, that has been latent all along. A kind of song with lyrics misheard that you half-remember at the end of a party to which you were not invited. Invite yourself to the party. Balloons and tunes and new friends found. Words will find you. Words know the address. Words will take the time to make time for the making that matters, which is their task and their talent. It is their favourite thing to do.

This is just something someone wrote by hand in the margins of a book.

Rite of Spring

He stepped into the garden
Slow motion in a new blue shirt
A lighter heart perhaps or something
Light here, light there
Something in the air
After a year of refusing kisses

Any intimacy
Once spoken
Loses elasticity

He hovered in the doorway
As if the day would last forever
Endless moments inside him
Nothing to be done
He unravelled there and then
And then

Intimacy

that long new year
we held it together
with tender attendance
unparalleled constancy
and i held it all so close to my chest
thinking it for the best
it remained unspoken

i blamed myself
and walked away
you did not notice
i did not look back
it was impossible to stay
i let you go / you let me go

In Front of Strangers I Sing Again

Some days these days I can't even
I can't even get out of bed
all the skin that's been shed
and still this mortal lump.

Did I do something wrong
or was I just there
whilst something wrong was happening?

Faceless and hopeless, I reach
for my own helpless hand in the night.

This moment is over.
That moment is over.
Here we go again.

Windfall

I am going to keep on writing it down
how you

Fort. Da.

for Tim

now and then I forget
and then remember
the shape of our bodies that night
mirrors and half-light
and a kind of kissing that was
nothing like kissing
more like tapestry or discovery

like sudden surprising snow
when it comes, changing the landscape,
gone in the morning, this tentative love
and a promise: to return, to repeat, to renew

to know always and forever that one
plus one makes more than two

Fort. Da. You.

Light Damage

Let me lie with you Andrew
And draw the evening close
Don't we know in our bones
That the moment has arrived
Inside us and are we ready at last
For the necessary task of welcoming impermanence?

Even apart and alone,
You were the alarm that woke me,
In a Mexican hotel, and called me home.

Now I am thanking you without thinking
Lost in a dream of what might have been

Your smile, all the while,
Is inside me, even if you're not.

Clearing

further a field
we walked
until tomorrow was
yesterday
look we were looking
and walking
smiling somehow because
we were still moving
our eyes full of light and
look I am loving you still
despite everything
because that means
something is moving in me

Slow Love

you were always the answer
to any question I had
seasons changed but you
were always the reason
for any task I undertook
even when I tired of you
the years passed by and
my love for you did not
expire, remained as fresh
as the day we met and
did not walk on by, we stayed
for the questions, found
ourselves in the answers,
made the best of a bad time,
time and again, but still
we survived, and here we are

Season Two

You have done all this
and I have done all this
and we have done all this
but there is still so much
more to do and so we ask:

What else is there to do?

Otherwise

It only took one look to love you
Then ten years to forget
Or not forget exactly but forgive
Myself for being so in need of love
That I'd invent it out of nothing

Not that you were nothing but
You weren't quite what I meant
You were altogether otherwise,
Unexpected, you were never mine

And if you have a moment, do me a favour,
remember me and how I thought of you:
incomparable, often, then. Or not at all.

Archaic Hurt

So many promises
Leading to nothing

There is no honour anymore
Nor anyone to do the honour to

I hope you find yourself alone
For a whole generation
And lose your way

I hope you've stopped taking your mother's advice

The Sad Night

Is this how a revolution happens?

A kiss on the hand
The quiet betrayal
History unravelling
Through the tender gesture

Lucky coincidence
Right man right year
Mistaken for a god
He made a history of us

Who was to blame?

A tuneless frequency
Through the longest night
Dead within days
Retreat and return

This is how a revolution happens

Anniversary

A wasted year of wasted days

All that time I watched you
But could not describe
What I had seen

All of my witnessing
Nought nought nought

I will not give us another thought.

Orison

When you found me it was later
and already I had lost
what once had made me shine

There was nothing new to love there

You took your fucking time

Remains

We knew they would come back some day,
Arriving in the morning post,
All the things we gave away.

The day turned plain after a time and
We no longer noticed when night came
Or the weather changed
And we ran out of things to say.

So many things remained unsaid.

We climbed into bed,
That endless night,
Hunting for language like dreams,
Or dreams that might speak,
And in the heavy silence made love,
Like a ladder through the night,
Love in the spaces between us,
Searching for heaven or somewhere
Dark to hide, a little like night
Or love or somewhere we had never been.

The Wild Runner

It's nice to stay in touch but is it really?

There was a list upon which your name did not appear.
That was another place, another year.
There was a wish made upon a long dead star.
I am sorry to have slept through your birthday.
It will never happen again.

I don't know how to love you now
Because I didn't love you then.

If I was hopeless then, I'm honest now.
I would have loved you more if I had known.

Peace Revels

I closed my eyes through Russell Square
I cut my hair
I cried on the night bus
I told a lie (to myself, for years)

I forgot your face, I forgot your name,
I could not forget the pain.
It was impossible to stay.

And if I loved you then,
then I was wrong. And love
was just a repetition undone
A misunderstanding
A wound unwound
Until

Becoming strange
we feel this world afresh
and live again.

Open City

Out of black waves
Days spit and splinter
Night overtakes (us here)

Lucid domes and shadow boats
Steady processions of preoccupied fire-flies

Here at the lit-up edge of a doorway
Opening onto this moving world still
Still turning, churning itself out,
Repeating reflections.

I could sit and watch for hours
The slow dark pulse of wave licking wave
As sky and water blur
And in between a strip of lights dance the horizon.

Little divides us from this
The whole world is split
Nudging each other's reality.

Everything is open.

Erosion

It is not the calendar or watch that tells the time here.
It is footfalls and breath on an empty staircase.
It is twelve tired nuns praying for morning.
It is the night when river and sky reverse.
It is – is it? – the opening and closing of doors.
It is the way the shadow of my skin can map itself against
Your skin, even after all these years.
It is last night and this morning.
It is a warning from history and a kind of mourning
For a time that cannot come again. But does of course.
It is the reading of these words, the giving voice,
and space, and silence too.
The breath.

Our quiet hearts audible at last.

This house he never saw complete.

She climbs the stairs to find him.

The Passing

It was a face that you had never seen
that greeted you on waking
from the dream of another life
(and another hand that took your hand
beneath the slowly changing sky).
So time will find a way to get inside you
and if you lose your shadow (again),
sew it on, live through the pain.
The waves that wait and the stars that shift,
the whole world holding breath to have you back.
This is the quiet carnival of life,
endlessly evolving back into itself,
repetitive devotion to the passing moment.
Everything is useful. Everything has its place.
It passes. It passes. It passes, you know.
Live through this and learn to love the changes.
Find your place in the range of being in the world.
It's passing still.

Wedding Poem

for Mariano & Jorge

When a voice inside you says: 'love this man'
you listen with your whole body
you answer with your heart.

This is how it begins
but the true art is making it last
the wildflowers of love growing wilder every day.

When everything you have ever known
is thrown into the air like so much confetti
his hand in your hand is everything you need.

When a love becomes a life we should all celebrate
night or day, whatever the weather
love is always, simply, everything, forever.

Chroma

for Derek Jarman

Before I knew you, I imagined you.
From brief descriptions in a catalogue,
I invented a world that I could step into,
and each step took me closer to myself.

Waking up at the edge of the library,
a copy of *Chroma* in my hands,
taking it with me, into the world,
and I remember the smell
of carpets and secrets,
and all that colour
it stained my life forever.

I imagined the story of a young man
in a coma, embraced by colour,
a bookmark for the heart.

I was asleep
and your book
it woke me with a kiss.

I think about you all the time.
These days I fall asleep in the cinema.
You do not have to see the film to get the feeling.

O Derek, with your rainbow of words,
have we lived the dreams you left for us?

Love Poem for The Kraken

below the thunders of the upper deep,
far, far beneath in the abysmal sea,
my lover sleeps and waits for me,
waiting for the time we'll meet again,
and in his many arms I'll find,
peace and siren's songs, so long, my lost
monster of many names, deep wet surprise,
covered in shells, organisms, birds,
across depth and height and width,
I love all that is deep and dark in you,
all the luck of the ocean floor,
secrets of the seabed,
endless, open, your arms enfold me
and then again and again and again

The Flying Dutchman

Everybody's haunted nowadays.
There is no getting away from
the spirit of the times, which is
to be all at sea, an absolute mood,
drifting forever through the wet doom.

Drifting is a really shit way to live -
I don't want to do it anymore -
and so I close my eyes to mirages
and your bad weather.

Sky and sea the same,
and if you're flying, I don't want to know,
It's all getting dimmer and I am almost done.

Thank you for your understanding at this difficult time.

The Garden God

Bedclothes in the topiary.
You wake up with the taste
of moss upon your lips
and stained knees again,
not sure where you have been.

Out of doors once more, barely aware
and wondering how this has happened
how it keeps on happening.
The smell of pine surrounds you
as you hide beneath the bush,
mouth full of twigs and green.

Another night, strange silences in moonlight.
The hour yet to be, so full of mystery.
Hope and the unknown.

This Evening Also

When every reflection was stolen
when every soul was shrunken
when every shard had settled.

The mirror and the broken pieces
rain or a tear in your eye
a tear in your sleeve and
something changed

This evening also you feel it,
although many years have passed,
and skins shed, feelings forgotten,
lives lived beyond their use, you feel it still.

...fragments of glass floating in the air...

And I can feel it too.

Orlando's Last Cry

We were not the last, but still the ending
made a deep impression on our love,
and how we lived our lives.
The love was long, but loose, and could not hold
beyond our individual fists of time.
Do not ask me what the time is.
I know only the stopped watch and time past.
Do not ask me if we are the first or – truly – the last.

We close the curtains on this broken day.

Expectation, you know, is death. Come back.
Come back to the present moment, yes back.
Back to this present moment, and love me again.
Love me now. Love me then. Again.

Now love as well has had its time
and so we close our hearts.
The holding open could not last.
Our pluck was over-priced.

What is the cost of love this time?

As if this year, this hour...

i.m. NH

Since you've been gone I
Think we've all been waiting
For something or someone
To explain the sudden change.

Minutes or millennia -
One moment to the next -
What difference does it make?
The quiet company of where you were.
And us, alone, inquisitive again.

Our faces give themselves away.
There will be tears in our mouths by morning.

Dream Language

when do mountains
how does language
why do people
who does nothing
where is nowhere

        and do they anyway

Reborn

Not a moment wasted
Each one reaching for the next
Such speed
No movement visible
Always saying ‘yes’

Found Text

Some things you never get used to

Fire

The world is almost always over
but somehow everything
is almost always fine.

Abasement

Even after everything
You've got to love yourself.
That's what it's all about!

Fragment of Promise (Borrowed)

I have wounds to show you,
which shall be yours in private.[1]

[1] Shakespeare, *Coriolanus* Act 2 Scene 3

from 'The Changes'

I know that it is difficult to love.
But love me. Love me. Love me.
Love me as I love you, or differently.
But do it. What else can you do?
Love me as space loves a curve,
as time loves a tense, as the universe adores variety.
Love me as the sky is blue, the sun is gold,
and even when the colours change,
keep on loving, because what else can you do?
Love me in the morning as the sun sets.
Love me in the evening as it rises.
Love me as the river rises. As my body rises to your touch.
Love me out of season, as the weather changes.
In all kinds of weather.
The love of our kind is unpredictable too.
Love me if you can.
Some things are not ours to decide.
I understand.
Love me as a field mouse after fire searches for a home.
Love me as a town mouse searches out a train.
Love me and love me again.

My love for you has changed.
Perhaps not the love, but I have changed.
The love has changed me.

Forgiveness

If you think this poem is for you,
then it is for you, using your body
the way it was meant – opening,
balancing, forever, yes, again

Exit Strategy

Eventually the lonely hour falls
The glacial moment melts
And you are left to reconcile
Everything you have ever known.

Now is the time to audit your many loves
And now the time to leave them all behind.

You will know it is time to leave
When your life wakes up
And reminds you who you are
Then leaves you, open and afraid.

Mutability

It did not have to end.
Any end is just another
moment of movement,
following the feeling,
as far as it goes, without
promise of meaning,
let's begin again.
It did not have to end.

Quotations

I have already left your city, already begun to move.

Two languages meet each other. They make a third.
This is the visible sifting of a shifting world.

My tongue stumbles again over strange coordinates.
It rewinds and finds itself amongst unspeakable loss.

Across the city multiplicity sings its many songs
Of both universe and void.

We no longer avoid the differences or distances
Between us. Every thing knows everything else.

Behind every poem is another poem
Let us begin with a quotation

Fallow We Lay

Life is only a moment, life too is only a dissolving
of ourselves in all others as by an act of giving:

Boris Pasternak

There are things one cannot render.

Emily Jeremiah

1

We did not come quietly,
bringing our lives,
bringing the world with us into the room.
What we wanted remaining unknown, even to ourselves.

Lying fallow
Fallow we lay
(Together we took our time)

The best thing about being invisible
is not having to think of anything to say.
I wanted to be less visible,
which does not mean I wanted to disappear.
Together we held the space.

Lying fallow
Fallow we lay
(Together we took our time)

That first afternoon we did not know
what would happen next,
or who we might become
in the spaces between each meeting.

Lying fallow
Fallow we lay
(Together we took our time)

Separate we came and left changed;
strangers not so strange.

Lying fallow
Fallow we lay
(Together we took our time)

Nameless and open
you could have been anyone
thank you for listening
and taking off your watch

Lying fallow
Fallow we lay
(Together we took our time)

Lay me down in Autumn leaves,
and leave me there
to find my own way
through the melting ground…

Lying fallow
Fallow we lay
(Together we took our time)

To be in the sudden silence of that room again,
with all of you,
awaiting the arrival
of our truest selves.

As Stella said: *This is real for some of us.*
And so it was.

2

We spent the day together
Alone we gathered
in preparation to disperse again

What was so radical
about the way you stood in a certain light
as we let the day slip by?

We asked the world to stop for a moment
so that we could see what it all might mean

We spent all day
A new understanding of time
A revelation at the edges of things

(forgive yourself the quiet now)

Forgetting and forgiving we got carried away
Just standing still we were upsetting the peace
It was a pain to be so untouched -
a shadow on our dreams
And how do we begin to wake?

Sweep me away; it's over; it has begun.

And that afternoon you were asleep at my feet
as I drew a vase of flowers
in this borrowed room

And that afternoon we went for our separate walks
finding our way back
through instinct and chance

And I can't stop thinking about a noisy man
who died a quiet death
and joined us in our circle

It was the first time I had let him in

All our dead were with us perhaps
in the questions we didn't ask

(This man who took my trauma to town
came back and sat with us
his mouth closed finally and his heart in his hands
I was able to look him in the eye
and take his hand in mine
I was able to begin to forgive
to start to put the fires out
now)

We made possible so many things
I loved us, even in our difficulty
I remember us fondly, even in my loss

In a closing park at dusk
we stood apart then together then apart
in love with the gathering dark
in silence then in speech and through beyond words

I ask:
What is the difference between a plane and a star?
All the while I have no idea who you are.

3

If I died this is what you'd find:
Me on my way, full of anxiety and anticipation.
Me arrived, taking my place, waiting for a sign.
Me sitting in a circle of strangers and I have never felt so held.
Me taking off my shoes before the feast.
Me learning my own name in a new language.
Me listening for my cue to breathe again.
Me meeting an old friend as if for the first time.
Me smiling at a stranger, willing them to *be okay.*
Me filled with the knowledge that we are always alone and
that is okay.
Me surprising myself.
I am learning to be done with questions, except:

What is this life that I call mine?

Shhh…

What if we waited?
What if we stopped hoping, started living instead?
What if the quiet was another name for noise?
What if we waited?

A stranger slept at my feet as I watched the light change across an afternoon.

Repeat.

Mary is trying to describe the experience.
She says *It is something I didn't know.*

Break it. Hold it. Know it and unknow it.

Put your expectations down.
Turn off anticipation.
Honour the moment.
Let it pass.

Take off your shoes and come into the room.
Not avoidance but confrontation.
The difficult moments that make it possible to grow.
The secret sharing that makes it possible to live.
The wild silences of love.
We did not know each other,
and then somehow we did.
This new kind of doing and waiting.
Thought + Presence + Time.

Let us not forget how fallow we were.
Oh how we lay.
What value there was in letting go.
Unforgettable light.

There was new life in the lost moment.
A fallow field full of promise.
An unfinished pile of leaves.
And when it was over then there was movement in a new direction too.

Now we sit in other rooms.
In changing light
We wait for the evening
To drown the sky outside.

I guess letting go is a new way to know
who we're going to be in the years left to live.

Somewhere we are watching the sun set still.
We are not finished yet.

Fallow We Lay was written in response to the experience of taking part in Rajni Shah Projects' *Lying Fallow*, a year-long project which explored through practice the concept and value of 'lying fallow' within the wider context of a society which is frequently driven by product, outcome, and the charade of efficiency. It was great.

Quiet Time

The moment when a feeling enters the body
is political. This touch is political.

Adrienne Rich

I am now quiet waiting for my visitor
it rains a little and I do not move
if only to make (notes for) this
(I will be) waiting for a while

Martin Corless-Smith

1

You do not have to be lonely.

In the smallest hours of the morning,
for a moment, could you see yourself
living here forever? The weather.

I dream of leaving the internet and taking a lover,
just getting on with it all, you know.

It is dark outside as I swim and my day begins.

The breathless banality of the body
of my quiet companion
at the swimming baths.
Later, in front of the mirrors, he combs his hair.
I cannot help but stare, knowing what is
covered by the cloth he wears.

Briefest charge of skin, shapes of imperfect flesh, no shame.

Again.

And if it's been a bad day already,
and the only way to change it is to go back,
then let's go back, yes let's go back.

Take off your shirt again, peel off your second skin,
and jump, jump, jump
Jump.
Right.
In.

The water is. The water it's. The water's fine.

About time.
In the failing light, I write these words.
An incantation.
This little water song.
A wet prayer for the passing day.
For you, who came so close, who comes back every day,
who holds your breath so effortlessly,
you've dived the fucking depths. It's cool.

2

Official descriptions were inadequate
for artworks whose own voices
were so strong they left us
speechless and alone.

In the museum courtyard
we watched the season change and change again
drinking hot chocolate we talked about old friends.

It was then that I realised
the truth of the trauma
it's sense and its scope.

There are moments I cannot forget or remember or whatever.

All questions have a limit.
There is no depth to questions, no hope.
Better build a fire instead.

The gallery emptied.

Imagine the empty rooms, the empty walls.
Imagine beginning again.

What would you hang and how?

It is late evening.
I prepare to make my daily report.
Which words will work tonight?

It's okay.

We come and go. Ours is a friendship
that trusts itself to part.
In this way the present is the past
and nothing really changes except
the expiry dates on the sandwiches we share.

The courtyard and the cold.
The sunlight and the smiles.
I don't need to tell you everything.
I don't need to tell you anything.
Because it's not, it's not, it's not about that now.
It never was.

In our silence is a song.

It does not end.

On a Tuesday afternoon in Piccadilly
I understood
the difference between truth and light.

What else was I there for?
Perhaps that was enough.

3

When you could not speak
When you could not speak
When you could not speak for days, for weeks
For months you could not move

Could you begin again?
Could you begin?
Not knowing what had happened
Except that nothing had and everything had
Not knowing what it meant
Not knowing who you were anymore
Nor who you had been, or how, or why

And then

4

I remember happiness, but I'm out of practice.
A journey home from France, through the night,
When I was still small enough to be loved.

Stopping for toast off the M25.
Was it the jam or the journey that made the moment live?

Memory is a pain.
You have to go long.
So long is time and pain a moment's work.

It all comes back in the end.

5

And so we breathe with others
In the chosen room,
Living bodies and a miracle of love,
an accident of friendship. Repeat.

Wait for the light to pass again.
Wait and the light will rise.
Wait until it goes again.
And wait.
Wait.
Wait.

(and I'm still waiting)

6

The way the light
The way the light was ready for us
The way the light made no explanation
The way the light moved
The way the light was generous
The way the light could compensate
The way the light was kind
The way the light revealed
The way the light could feel
The way the light made light of things
The way the light undid
The way the light repaired
The way the light forgave
The way the light forgot
The way the light spread
The way the light spoke
The way the light sang
The way the light slipped
The way the light danced
The way the light reached out
The way the light gave way
The way the light was me
The way the light was you
The way the light was us
The way the light
These have been difficult times
and still the light.

7

Do not hesitate to take up space.
It is a way of being generous to the world.
It is a way of saying yes.
It is an open door through which
the world welcomes you.
It is an invitation, a reminder and reiteration,
a special dietary requirement.
It is just another moment to remember or forget.
It is forgiving in its repetition.
It is a fresh translation of the day.
Your moving hand, the blank white page.
It is impossible to say just yet
what the meaning might be
or what marks might remain when the moment has moved on.

I sit with my friend in a café on Tottenham Court Road,
and because I love him I say:
Don't worry. Just keep writing. It's okay.

And on we go.

Source Notes

The cover image is 'Pensador' by Daniel El Dibujo (www.eldibujo.com)

Dedication from 'Let Me Count the Ways,' words and music by Yoko Ono, © 1984 (from the album *Milk & Honey*).

Dedication from 'My Teacher Died,' words and music by Diane Cluck, © 2005 (from the album *Countless Times*), reproduced by permission of the artist.

Epigraph from 'Late Echo' by John Ashbery, from *As We Know*, Viking Press, 1979. Used by permission of Carcanet Press Limited.

Epigraph from 'The Touch' by Anne Sexton, from *Love Poems*, Oxford University Press, 1979. Reprinted by permission of SLL/Sterling Lord Literistic, Inc. © Linda Gray Sexton.

Epigraph from *The Language of Inquiry* by Lyn Hejinian, University of California Press, 2000.

Love Poem for The Kraken emerges from Alfred Tennyson's 1830 poem *The Kraken*.

The Garden God is inspired by the 1906 novel of the same name by Forrest Reid.

'Some Things You Never Get Used To' was a 1968 release for The Supremes. It never tires. What can I say? Some things you never get used to.

'Fragment of Promise (Borrowed)' is composed of a quotation from William Shakespeare's *Coriolanus,* Act 2 Scene 3.

The final line of *Quotations* is itself a quotation from the first line of Italo Calvino's essay 'Multiplicity,' which appears in *Six Memos for the Next Millenium*. Copyright © 2002, The Estate of Italo Calvino, used by permission of The Wylie Agency (UK) Limited.

'The Wedding Party,' by Boris Pasternak. Translated by Edwin Morgan, from *Collected Translations*, 1996. Used by permission of Carcanet Press Limited.

Epigraph by Emily Jeremiah reproduced by permission of the author.

Epigraph from *Nota*, by Martin Corless-Smith, Fence Books, 2003.
Reproduced by permission of the author.

Epigraph from 'The Blue Ghazals', by Adrienne Rich, in
The Will to Change: Poems 1968-1970, Norton, 1971.

Ben Webb is a queer writer based in London, making formally playful, poetic works of art for assorted audiences. Work for theatre includes a trilogy of gay plays: *So Little of You Left, His Spread Legs* and *The Actor Has Told of His Pain* (collected as *The Well & Badly Loved* and published by Bloomsbury). *The Well & Badly Loved* has been translated into Spanish and French and performed in London, Lyon, Paris and Mexico City. Writing for film includes *Lightly Covered with Buttoned Cloth*, a triptych of films directed by Poppie Sköld (*Our Life Together, Envoi* and *The Present Day*). Ben is currently working on a new collection of poems as well as an oral history of the uncredited dancing sailors from Derek Jarman's 1979 film of *The Tempest*.

WWW.RISKINGENCHANTMENT.COM

Printed in Great Britain
by Amazon

46760177R00046